Fiona
the Flute
Fairy

Special thanks to

Narinder Dhami

ISBN: 978-0-545-10626-9

12 11 10 9 8 7 6 5 4 3 2 1   10 11 12 13 14 15/0

Printed in the U.S.A.

First Scholastic Printing, January 2010

Fiona
the Flute
Fairy

by Daisy Meadows

LITTLE APPLE

SCHOLASTIC INC.

New York   Toronto   London   Auckland
Sydney   Mexico City   New Delhi   Hong Kong

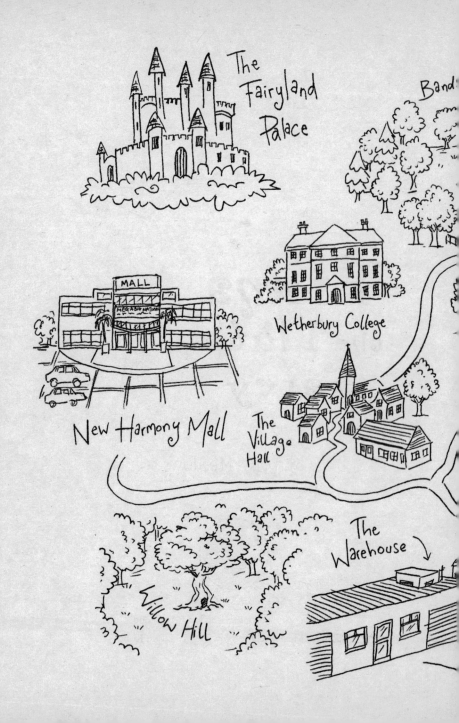

I'm through with frost, ice, and snow.
To the human world I must go!
I'll form my cool Gobolicious Band.
Magical instruments will lend a hand.

With these instruments, I'll go far.
Frosty Jack, a superstar.
I'll steal music's harmony and its fun.
Watch out, world, I'll be number one!

Contents

Card Trick

"Oh, this is one of my favorite stores in Wetherbury!" Rachel Walker stopped outside Sparkly Wishes and turned to her best friend, Kirsty Tate. "They always have such fabulous cards and gifts. Can we go in?"

"OK," Kirsty agreed, pushing open the

door. "Do you want to buy something, or just look around?"

"I want to get a thank-you card to give your parents when I go home at the end of school break," Rachel replied, heading inside.

Kirsty smiled. "Oh, that's so nice, Rachel!"

"I'll get a card to send to Mom and Dad, too," Rachel went on, "just to say that I'm fine and having a great time." She grinned. "Although my parents know that I *always* have a great time when I stay with you, Kirsty."

"They don't know that we're friends with the fairies and have lots of exciting, magical adventures, though!" Kirsty pointed out in a whisper.

Rachel nodded. The Music Fairies had asked for the girls' help after Jack Frost and his mischievous goblins had stolen the seven magic musical instruments from the Fairyland School of Music. These special instruments made music fun and harmonious in both the human and fairy worlds. Without them, music everywhere sounded terrible and out of tune!

Rachel and Kirsty had been horrified to discover that Jack Frost had plans to use the instruments' magical powers to win the National Talent Competition at the New Harmony Mall near Wetherbury. Jack Frost was determined to win first place and get a recording contract with MegaBig Records. He had sent his goblins to hide in Wetherbury with the magic instruments, so they'd be ready for the competition that weekend. But, with the help of the Music Fairies, the girls were determined to foil his plans and return all of the instruments to Fairyland before Rachel went home at the end of school break.

"I hope we find another instrument today," Rachel said, as she flipped through a display of glittery cards. "We've

already helped send Poppy's piano
and Ellie's guitar back to Fairyland,
but we still need to find all the other
instruments so music isn't ruined
forever!"

"I know," Kirsty
agreed. "But remember
what Queen Titania
always says? We
have to let the
magic come to *us*."

"It's hard though,
isn't it?" Rachel sighed.

"*Really* hard!" Kirsty agreed.

She left Rachel alone so she could
choose her cards, and went over to look
at a shelf of cute teddy bears. There
weren't any other customers in the store,
except for a little boy and his mother.

Kirsty wandered around, looking at
whatever caught her eye.

Suddenly she spotted a large, bright
card at the front of a nearby display.
The card was covered with silver
sparkles. In the middle was a pretty
little fairy with long red hair.

She looks like Poppy the Piano Fairy!
Kirsty thought, smiling to herself.

Kirsty took the card to show Rachel,

who was looking at postcards of different
Wetherbury sights.

"Does this remind you of anyone,
Rachel?" asked Kirsty, holding the
card out.

"Oh, yes! Poppy!" Rachel exclaimed.
"Maybe I should send that card to my
mom and dad. What does it say inside?"

Kirsty flipped the card open.
Immediately, a puff of glitter burst out,
showering both girls
with sparkles. Rachel and
Kirsty gasped as a
tiny fairy
popped out of
the card and
waved at them.
She wore a shiny

silver dress with lace-up sandals, and
her dark hair was braided with pretty
beads.

"Hi, girls," she called. "I'm Fiona the
Flute Fairy!"

"We're so glad to see you, Fiona,"
Rachel said eagerly.

"Do you think your magic flute is
nearby?" asked Kirsty.

Fiona nodded seriously.
"And I hope you'll help
me find it," she said.
"There's no time to waste!
Did you know that Jack
Frost and his goblins are going
to enter the National Talent
Competition next weekend?"

"Oh, yes." Rachel grinned.

"We've heard all
about Frosty
and his
Gobolicious
Band!"

Fiona smiled.
"We've heard
rumors in
Fairyland that Jack Frost is writing his
own songs for the competition," she told
them. "So far, he's got 'You've Got to
Be Cold to Be Kind,' 'Green with
Envy,' and 'Fairyland Rock'!"

The girls laughed.

"I wonder what his songs are like?"
said Rachel.

"Even if they're *awful*," Fiona replied,
"Jack Frost will still win the talent

competition with the help of the magic
musical instruments!"

"Then he'll get the recording contract
with MegaBig Records," Kirsty pointed
out. "If he becomes a famous pop star,
everyone will want to know all
about him."

"And that would mean disaster for
Fairyland!" Fiona sighed, her wings
drooping a little. "You understand that

we can't let *anyone* find out
about fairies. Girls, we
have to stop Jack Frost!"

"Well, let's start by
looking for your flute,"
Kirsty said in a
determined voice.

"It's not far away, I
know it!" Fiona replied,

fluttering down to sit on Kirsty's shoulder.
"I can feel its beautiful music calling
to me."

Rachel was about to say something
when a movement outside the window
caught her eye. Suddenly, a large group
of people danced past the card store!

Follow the Music!

Amazed, Rachel rubbed her eyes. Was she seeing things?

She peeked outside with curiosity. The dancers were moving down High Street. There was a painter still holding his wet brush, which left a trail of green paint behind him as he twirled around a lamppost.

A mother with a stroller was skipping along, her baby giggling with delight. A man in a suit was waltzing and talking into his cell phone at the same time.

"Kirsty!" Rachel tugged her friend's sleeve. "You *have* to see this!"

Kirsty looked up. "What's happening?" she asked, puzzled.

At that moment, the little boy in the store, who was looking at the display of teddy bears, glanced outside and spotted the dancers.

"Look, Mom, it's a parade!" he yelled excitedly.

"Let's go and watch," his mom replied. They hurried out of the card store, leaving the door open behind them. Immediately, the sound of sweet, melodic music drifted in from the street.

"What beautiful music!" Rachel said dreamily. "What's the parade for, Kirsty?"

"I don't know," Kirsty replied, swaying in time to the music. "I had no idea there

was going to be a parade in Wetherbury today."

"Girls, listen to me!" Fiona said anxiously. But Rachel and Kirsty didn't even look at her.

"I *have* to find out where this amazing music is coming from!" Rachel went on, heading for the door.

"I know it's strange, but there's just *something* about this music," Kirsty agreed. "I *need to* follow it!" She rushed after Rachel.

"That's just it, girls!" Fiona darted in front of them, blocking their path. "This beautiful music is coming from my magic flute!"

Rachel and Kirsty stared at her.

"People can't resist the sweet sounds of my flute, and that means it could be dangerous in the wrong hands," Fiona explained quickly.

She waved her wand to break the spell the flute had cast over the girls.

"We have to get it back, then," said Rachel, giving herself a little shake.

Fiona swooped into Rachel's pocket and the three friends rushed outside. High Street was now crowded with people dancing around. Even the cars had stopped! Their drivers had gotten out to join in the fun.

"The music's getting fainter." Fiona looked worried. "That means whoever has my flute is moving farther away. I'll turn you both into fairies, so we can fly after them."

Rachel and Kirsty hurried into a nearby phone booth.

Fiona flew out of Rachel's pocket and quickly showered both girls with a cloud of shimmering sparkles. Instantly, Kirsty and Rachel shrank down to fairy-size, with glittery wings on their shoulders.

"Let's go!" Fiona cried, soaring out of the phone booth.

Rachel and Kirsty followed, and the three friends zoomed along High Street. They kept well above the heads of the dancing crowds and followed the faint, sweet melody of the flute.

"We should be on the lookout for goblins," Kirsty said. "Remember that

Jack Frost's spell has made them look
more like people."

"Yes, they aren't green anymore,"
Rachel agreed as they wove their way
between the street lights. "But the spell
didn't work completely, so we can still
recognize them by their big noses, ears,
and feet!"

"The music's getting louder again,"
Fiona said, looking
around. Suddenly,
she gave a gasp of
delight. "There's
my flute!"
Rachel and Kirsty
saw a little girl in a
pink party dress and
matching hat. She

was skipping
along, playing
the magic
flute. The
beautiful tune
brought people
out of the stores
and into the street,
dancing as the little
girl passed by.
"After her!" Rachel
cried, but Kirsty caught her arm.
"Wait!" she said. "Who are *they*?" She
pointed down at two strange-looking
boys chasing the little girl.

Their large noses and ears poked out
from under their baseball caps, and their
sneakers looked very big. They were

arguing loudly as they raced after the
girl, but the three fairy friends couldn't
hear exactly what they were saying.

"Goblins!" Rachel gasped.

"We have to stop them from stealing
my flute from the little girl!" Fiona
exclaimed.

Fiona, Rachel, and Kirsty hovered
above the girl, then ducked down to hide
behind the white daisies on her pink hat.
Rachel peeked cautiously over the hat's
brim at the little girl's face.

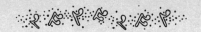

"Look at that big nose and those pointy ears!" Rachel whispered. "That's no little girl with the magic flute — that's a goblin!"

Tug of War!

Fiona and Kirsty leaned forward to look, but Fiona's shimmery wings tickled the goblin's ear. Annoyed, he swatted her away. The fairy tumbled off the hat.

"Fiona, are you OK?" Rachel asked anxiously, as she and Kirsty rushed out from behind the daisies.

"I'm fine!" Fiona panted, pausing in midair to give her crumpled wings a shake.

"Look out! Fairy alert!" roared a gruff voice.

Disappointed, Fiona, Rachel, and Kirsty looked around. The boy goblins were rushing toward them, yelling loudly.

Fiona grabbed Kirsty's and Rachel's hands and pulled them to a nearby tree, where they hid among the leaves.

The "girl" goblin lowered the flute and glared at the other two.

"Stop shouting!" he grumbled. "You're interrupting my beautiful music!"

"But we saw *fairies* —" the bigger boy goblin began.

"Don't be silly!" snapped the "girl" goblin, glancing around. Because the music had stopped, the people had stopped dancing, too. The crowd was beginning to break up. "There are no

fairies here!" He eyed the other two goblins suspiciously. "I thought my disguise might fool you, but I know what you're up to," he went on. "You just want to steal my magic flute!"

"Well, now that you mention it . . ." the

smallest goblin said playfully. Then he
lunged forward, grabbing one end of the
flute. "Let me have it!"

"No way!" yelled the other goblin,
holding on to the mouthpiece of the flute
for dear life.

The girls watched in horror as the two
goblins began playing tug of war with
Fiona's flute.

"The flute's breaking!" Kirsty exclaimed. "They're ripping it apart!"

"Don't worry," Fiona explained quickly. "Flutes are *meant* to come apart. They are made in three pieces!"

As the goblins pulled harder, the flute broke into sections. The two goblins were left with a piece each, and the middle section clattered to the ground. The third goblin snatched it up immediately.

"Now we *all* have a flute!" he boasted. He put the piece to his lips, and the goblin with the end piece did the same. But when they blew into them, nothing happened.

"You fools!" The "girl" goblin snickered, holding up the mouthpiece. "You can't play a flute without *this*!"

The other two goblins sprang at him. He dodged them and dashed off, still laughing. Scowling, the others raced after him.

Rachel, Kirsty, and Fiona flew after the goblins. But they found it difficult to keep up with them, because they had to keep ducking and diving to make sure they weren't spotted by any of the shoppers.

"We can't lose them!" Rachel panted as the goblins raced past the Wetherbury Museum.

"They're going toward Willow Hill!" Kirsty cried as the goblins swerved away from High Street and headed out into the countryside.

"Perfect!" Fiona replied. "We'll be able to fly faster once we're out of the village

and don't have to worry about being spotted."

The goblins had all kicked off their shoes so that they could run even faster, but the "girl" goblin was still wearing his dress, wig, and hat. Now they rushed into the woods on Willow Hill. Fiona, Rachel, and Kirsty zoomed through the trees after them, speeding up since it was finally safe to do so. It didn't take them long to reach the goblins.

"Give me back my flute!" Fiona demanded.

The goblins were so startled, they almost jumped out of their skins!

"Fairies!" they screeched, and immediately took off in three different directions.

"Which way should we go?" Kirsty cried.

"We'll take one at a time," Fiona decided quickly. "That one first!" She pointed at the goblin who held the end section of the flute.

The goblin was weaving his way in and out of the trees, the end piece clutched firmly in his hand. Fiona, Rachel, and Kirsty raced after him.

"Why don't you just give up?" Rachel yelled. "You're no match for the three of us!"

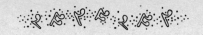

The goblin chuckled. "Actually," he said smugly, twisting around to look at Rachel, "three silly fairies are no match for *me!*"

The goblin was so busy boasting and bragging that he didn't watch where he was going. There was a log in his path, and he tripped right over it, going head-over-heels with a loud shriek.

As he fell, the goblin lost his grip on the flute piece. It flew from his hand and sailed through the air!

Double Trouble

"Quick!" Fiona cried.

She and the girls rushed toward the end section of the flute as it tumbled downward. Between the three of them, they managed to catch it before it hit the ground. Then, with a whisk of Fiona's wand, a puff of glittering magic dust shrank the piece back to Fairyland size.

"We'd better see if the goblin is OK," said Rachel.

Luckily, the goblin had landed in a soft pile of leaves. As Rachel hovered above the pile, the goblin crawled out, dusting himself off and muttering angrily. But Rachel thought she was seeing things when a *second* goblin also popped his head out of the leaves!

"Oh, no!" she called to Kirsty and Fiona. "The goblins are multiplying!"

"You landed right in the middle of my hiding place!" shouted the second goblin furiously.

"You be quiet!" screeched the first goblin. The two of them began to wrestle, sending the leaves whirling in all directions.

"Just give the second piece of the flute to us!" said Kirsty.

The goblins stopped wrestling and stared down at their hands in panic.

"I don't have my flute piece!" groaned the first goblin.

"I don't have mine, either!" added the second one. "You stole it!"

"No, I didn't!" the first goblin declared. As the goblins began arguing again, Rachel suddenly spotted a gleam of silver among the fallen leaves. "Fiona, I think the missing piece is down there, hidden under the leaves!" she whispered. "But how will we get to it?"

"Leave it to me," Fiona said. She pointed her wand at the leaves and began to sing:

"Pretty leaves,
orange and gold,
lie fallen on
the ground.
When you hear
my magical song,
rise up and
dance around!"

Immediately, the leaves rose up in a colorful cloud and began to swirl around the two goblins.

"Help!" the first goblin yelled.
He swatted at the leaves
and accidentally
smacked the second
goblin on the nose.

"Ow!" the second
goblin roared,
jumping up and
down with rage.

"There's the
second piece of
flute!" Rachel
whispered.

She pointed to
where the middle
section of the flute
rested uncovered on the
grass. Immediately, Fiona,
Rachel, and Kirsty swooped

down, and a wave of Fiona's
wand transformed it back to
Fairyland size. The goblins
were still trying to fight
their way out of the
whirlwind of leaves,
so Fiona and
the girls quickly
flew away.
"Two down, one
to go!" Fiona
smiled as she
fastened the pieces
together. "Now,
where's the goblin
who has the
mouthpiece?"
"He can't be far
away," Kirsty replied.

But the goblin seemed to have disappeared. Fiona and the girls hunted high and low, behind trees and under bushes, but the goblin was nowhere to be found.

"What do we do now?" asked Kirsty. Fiona glanced up into one of the trees where a squirrel sat, gnawing on a nut. "Maybe we need some help," she replied.

Curious, Kirsty and Rachel watched as Fiona pursed her lips and whistled a short, magical tune.

"Now ask the squirrel if he's seen the goblin," Fiona said.

Rachel cleared her throat.

"Excuse me," she called. "We're looking for a goblin. Have you seen him?"

The squirrel stopped gnawing and looked down at Rachel.

"I'm afraid I haven't seen anyone," he replied. "Except you! Sorry I can't be of more help."

Fiona had used her magic so that the girls could speak with the animals!

"I haven't seen any goblins, either!" chirped a bluebird that was nesting higher up in the tree.

"Thank you," Rachel said with an astonished smile.

Kirsty heard a rustling noise and spotted two rabbits in the bushes.

"Can you help us, please?" she asked. "We're looking for a goblin."

"Oh, we haven't seen anyone," the rabbits replied politely, before hopping off across the grass. "Sorry!"

"Let's try a different part of the woods," Fiona said.

As they flew deeper into the forest, a flash of dark orange caught Rachel's eye. A fox was sitting by a large bush.

"Let's ask that fox if he's seen the goblin," Rachel suggested. But as they swooped down, they could see that the fox looked very upset.

"Hello there," Fiona called. "What's wrong?"

The fox let out a heavy sigh. "Someone stole my den," he explained. "I built a cozy home among the roots of a big oak tree. I left, just for a minute, and now someone's stolen it!"

"Do you know who?" Kirsty asked sympathetically.

The fox shook his head. "No," he barked. "All I know is that a big blob

wedged itself in my den. It won't come out, and I can't get in!"

Fiona and the girls glanced at one another.

"Does this blob have a big nose?" asked Kirsty.

"And pointy ears?" said Rachel.

"And big feet?" Fiona added.

"Yes," the fox said. "And it's carrying a shiny stick."

"It's the goblin!" Rachel laughed.

Goblin in a Den

"Can you take us to your home?" Fiona asked the fox. "We might be able to get it back for you!"

The fox nodded eagerly and trotted off across the clearing. He led Fiona and the girls over to a large, sturdy oak tree and pointed his paw at a hole under its trunk.

"Look!" the fox said. Rachel, Kirsty, and Fiona couldn't help laughing. There, sticking out of the entrance to the fox's den, were two large, dirty goblin feet!

"Does the den have a back door?" asked Kirsty.

The fox trotted around the side of the tree and showed Fiona and the girls another entrance.

"Wait here," said Fiona to the fox. Then she, Rachel, and Kirsty flew inside.

The goblin was hunched inside the fox's den, groaning to himself. It was much too small for him! He looked cramped and uncomfortable.

"What are you pesky fairies doing here?" he demanded with a scowl.

"We've come to ask you to leave the fox's den, please!" said Fiona.

"It isn't nice to go into someone's house uninvited," added Rachel.

"I would leave if I could, but I can't!" the goblin replied. "I came in here to hide from *you*, but now I'm stuck — and my pretty dress is ruined!"

"We'll help you get out if you give us your piece of the flute," Kirsty offered, trying not to laugh.

The goblin frowned. "But it plays such pretty music!" he said. Suddenly he began to squirm around and giggle. "That fox is nipping at my feet again," he chuckled. "It tickles. Make him stop!"

"Only if you give us the mouthpiece," Rachel said firmly.

"Hee, hee!" the goblin laughed, wriggling around. "All right."

With a little effort, he managed to lift his arm and pass the mouthpiece to Fiona.

"Thank you!" said Fiona. "Now we'll try to get you out."

The three friends flew out of the den again. With a sprinkle of fairy dust, the mouthpiece shrank immediately and Fiona attached it to the rest of her flute.

"As good as new!" she said, giving it a kiss.

"Could you stop nipping at the goblin's feet?" Kirsty asked the fox. "If he stops wiggling around, maybe we can get him out of your den."

"I'm sure we can," Fiona added. "Girls, if I make you human-size again, you can pull him out by his feet!"

Rachel and Kirsty nodded. With one wave of Fiona's wand, they instantly zoomed back to their normal size.

Just as the girls were about to take hold of the goblin's feet, the other two goblins suddenly wandered into the clearing. They burst out laughing when they saw feet sticking out of the fox's den.

"What's he doing?" the biggest goblin snickered.

"He's stuck, and we're just about to  pull him out," Kirsty explained. The goblins laughed even louder. "Here goes!" Rachel said, grasping one of

the goblin's feet. "Oh, what is that horrible smell?"

"It's the goblin's stinky feet!" Kirsty groaned, holding her nose with one hand as she pulled on his other foot.

"I heard that!" the goblin in the den shouted angrily.

The girls pulled as hard as they could, but the goblin didn't budge. The other goblins thought it was hilarious. They danced around the tree, singing:

"Goblin in a den,
and he can't get out.
Jack Frost will be angry.
He'll scream and shout!"

Fiona lifted her flute to her lips. "I think it's time for some musical magic!" she exclaimed.

Magical Melody

Fiona began to play her flute. As the
sweet, soothing notes drifted around the
clearing, some of the woodland animals
popped out of their homes to listen. Even
the goblins fell silent.

Just then, Kirsty
noticed that the oak
tree was shaking
and shuddering. She
nudged Rachel.
"Look at the
tree!" she
whispered.
"It's *dancing*!"
Rachel gasped,
her eyes wide.
The tree was
swaying its branches in
time to the music. As it did, it rose up a
few inches, almost as if it were standing
on tiptoe.

"Pull, Rachel!" Kirsty cried, grasping
one of the goblin's feet tightly.

When the tree lifted up a little, the fox's den became slightly bigger. Both girls pulled as hard as they could on the goblin's feet. Suddenly, he shot out of the den like a cork from a bottle.

Fiona stopped playing and the tree's trunk dropped down again. Meanwhile, the goblin climbed to his feet and scowled at his friends.

"I heard you laughing at me!" he snapped.

"Where's your piece of the flute?" the big goblin demanded.

"I had to give it to those pesky fairies to get me out of the den!" the other goblin muttered.

"You fool!" the two goblins yelled.

"Well, where are *your* pieces?" the first goblin demanded, brushing off his dress.

The other two looked embarrassed.

"*She's* got them!" they exclaimed at once, pointing at Fiona.

"So who's the fool *now*?" the goblin in the dress argued. And the three goblins stomped off, squabbling all the way.

"Thank you for your help," the fox
said happily, sitting down in the doorway
of his den.

Fiona smiled and played another short
burst of the magical melody on her flute.
"My music will make sure you and your
family will always be happy in your den,"
she explained.

Then she turned to Rachel and Kirsty.
"Girls, thanks to you we have another
one of our precious magic musical
instruments back where it belongs!" she

said happily. "I must take my flute to Fairyland now, but I know you'll do your very best to find the other instruments. We just have to stop Jack Frost from winning the talent competition!"

"We will!" Rachel and Kirsty promised. Then, in a dazzle of glitter, Fiona vanished. She left a faint, sweet melody behind her. Whistling Fiona's tune, Rachel and Kirsty hurried back to High Street.

"Everything's back to normal," Rachel said, watching people going in and out of the stores.

"Yes, but imagine how much chaos there'll be if Frosty and his Gobolicious Band win the talent competition!" Kirsty pointed out. "Even if he only has *one* of the magic instruments, Jack Frost will still win."

"Then we've just *got* to find the other four instruments before this weekend," Rachel said seriously. "And then we can make sure that music is fun and harmonious again — for *everyone*!"

THE MUSIC FAIRIES

Fiona the Flute Fairy's magic instrument
is safe and sound in Fairyland! Can
Rachel and Kirsty help

Danni
the Drum Fairy?

Join their next adventure in this special
sneak peek!

Extra-Exciting

"Bye, girls. I'll see you later," said Mrs. Tate. "Have fun!"

"We will," Kirsty Tate replied, smiling. She leaned through the car window to kiss her mom good-bye. "Thanks for the ride. Bye!"

"Good-bye!" echoed Rachel Walker, Kirsty's best friend.

Both girls waved as Mrs. Tate drove away. Kirsty looked up at the warehouse building they were standing in front of, and grinned at Rachel. "What are we waiting for?" she said. "Let's get inside!"

Rachel's eyes were bright as she slipped an arm through one of Kirsty's. "I can't believe we're actually going to be in a music video!" she said happily. "As if this vacation wasn't already fun enough!"

The two girls walked through tall glass double doors into the warehouse, feeling bubbly with anticipation. Rachel was staying with Kirsty's family for a week over school break, and on the very first day the girls had found themselves in another one of their wonderful fairy adventures. This time, they were helping the Music Fairies find their magic

musical instruments, which had been stolen by Jack Frost and his goblins. So far, the girls had helped the Music Fairies find three of the instruments, but there were still four missing. . . .

RAINBOW magic™

There's Magic in Every Series!

The Rainbow Fairies

The Weather Fairies

The Jewel Fairies

The Pet Fairies

The Fun Day Fairies

The Petal Fairies

The Dance Fairies

Read them all!

📖 SCHOLASTIC

www.scholastic.com

www.rainbowmagiconline.com

HIT entertainment

RMFAIRY

RAINBOW magic
THE JEWEL FAIRIES

They Make Fairyland Sparkle!

SCHOLASTIC
www.scholastic.com
www.rainbowmagiconline.com

HIT entertainment

JEWEL

SPECIAL EDITION

Three Books in One!
More Rainbow Magic Fun!

■SCHOLASTIC
www.scholastic.com
www.rainbowmagiconline.com

HiT entertainment

RMSPECIAL2

RAINBOW magic

These activities are magical!
Play dress-up, send friendship notes, and much more!

SCHOLASTIC
www.scholastic.com
www.rainbowmagiconline.com

HiT entertainment

RMACTIV2

Come flutter by Butterfly Meadow!

#1: Dazzle's First Day

#2: Twinkle Dives In

#3: Three Cheers for Mallow!

#4: Skipper to the Rescue

#5: Dazzle's New Friend

#6: Twinkle and the Busy Bee

#7: Joy's Close Call

#8: Zippy's Tall Tale

#9: Skipper Gets Spooked